This is Bird.

Bird is a bird.

Birds get chased by kittens.

'Hello, Bird,' said Max. 'Let's be friends!'

'Yes, please!' said Bird.

'First, I'll chase you,' said Max.

'Then *maybe* I'll eat you up.

You look like a tasty snack!'

Max
and Bird

by Ed Vere

PUFFIN

This is Max.

Max is a kitten.

Kittens chase birds.

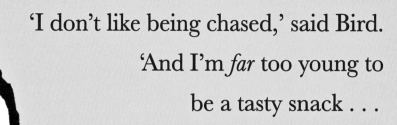

'I don't like being chased,' said Bird.
'And I'm *far* too young to
be a tasty snack . . .

I haven't **even** learnt to fly yet.'

'Oh,' said Max. 'But it's a rule of nature.
Birds get chased by kittens.'

'But friends don't eat each
other up!' said Bird.

'Hmm,' said Max. 'We need to think about this.'

Max and Bird sat and thought awhile.

'Hold on,' said Bird.

'I have an idea!'

Bird explained the principles
of friendship to Max.

'Friends have fun together
and help each other out . . .

'If you teach me how to fly,' said Bird,
'then we'll talk about the chasing . . .

. . . and all that *other* stuff. OK?'

'That,' said Max, 'is a very fair plan.'
They shook on the deal.

Max explained the principles of flight to Bird.

'Well, Bird, first of all, you . . . er . . .
What you do is . . .
Well . . .

. . . ahem,' coughed Max.

'I don't think I know how to fly either.'

'Follow me,' said Bird. 'We'll go to the library . . .

Libraries know everything.'

In the library there was a section on flying.

Max and Bird couldn't reach
the books on the top shelf . . .

AMELIA EARHART

LINDBERG

NAVIGATION

PLANES

AIR

READING THE SKY

GRAVITY

PACIFIC ISLANDS

CLOUDS

BLUE YONDER

FLYING

EARHART

KITES

OVER THE HORIZON

BE A BIRD

ISLAND HOPPING

TO FLY

THE RIGHT STUFF

. . . so they borrowed some
from the bottom.

Max and Bird studied for weeks.

They read important books
until their tiny brains were full.

To cut a long story short,
you just need to . . .

1. Concentrate hard.

2. Stick out your wings.

3. Flap.

Piece of cake!

Max and Bird concentrated hard.
They stuck out their *wings* . . .

And they flapped.

Nothing happened.

They flapped in the morning.

Not a bean.

They flapped in the afternoon.

Not a sausage.

They flapped in the evening.

Zilch.

Max and Bird were tired out.
All night long they slept.

All night long they dreamt of flying.

The next day, with heads full of dreams,
Max and Bird tried again . . .

They flapped
and flapped
until they ached.

NOTHING
happened.

Bird flipped, Bird stamped, Bird YELLED.

'NO FUN!
I'm bored,
BORED,
BORED!

Flapping isn't
working out.'

'Calm down,' said Max. 'We'll ask someone
who **can** fly. They'll tell us what to do.'

Max and Bird asked Pigeon
(very politely),
'Excuse us, could you *please*
    tell us how to fly . . .

        please?'

'Ha ha!' Pigeon cackled (rudely).
'Don't you **even** know how to fly?
    It's SO easy!
        Just stick out your wings
        And flap.

    Look . . .'

Pigeon flapped.

Pigeon flew upside down.

Pigeon zigged.

Pigeon zagged.

Pigeon looped the loop.

Pigeon was showing off.

With iron resolve, Max and Bird tried once more.

They flapped

and flapped . . .

. . . and flapped.

At 5.23 p.m. precisely, something
incredible happened . . .

It was wobbly, but Bird took off for
1, 2, **3** whole seconds!

'HURRAY!
We did it!'

'Thank you for teaching me
to fly,' said Bird.

'That's what friends are for,' said Max.

'Well, a deal's a deal,' said Bird.
'I suppose you want to eat me up now?'

'Oh,' said Max.
'*A tasty snack . . .*

I'd forgotten about that.
Let me have a think.'

Max had a think . . .

(Quite a long think.)

'I don't want to eat you up,' said Max.
'It's not what friends do . . .

But can I watch you fly instead please, Bird?'

'YES!' said Bird.

And he did his first loop-the-loop.

for
David & Jan

PUFFIN BOOKS
UK | USA | Canada | Ireland | Australia | India | New Zealand | South Africa
Puffin Books is part of the Penguin Random House group of companies
whose addresses can be found at global.penguinrandomhouse.com.
puffinbooks.com
First published 2016
001
Text and illustrations copyright © Ed Vere, 2016
The moral right of the author/illustrator has been asserted
Printed in China
A CIP catalogue record for this book is available from the British Library
Hardback ISBN: 978–0–723–29458–0
Paperback ISBN: 978–0–241–24019–9

edvere.com
@ed_vere